Adventures of Robin Hood

Retold by Rob Lloyd Jones

Illustrated by Alan Marks

Reading Consultant: Alison Kelly
Roehampton University

Contents

Chapter 1	Not just any outlaw	3
Chapter 2	The Sheriff's plan	12
Chapter 3	Tournament day	21
Chapter 4	The treasure room	30
Chapter 5	Thieves in the night	36
Chapter 6	Hanging day	42
Chapter 7	How Robin did it	54

Chapter 1

Not just any outlaw

"Pay up! Pay up!"

The shrill cry rang around Sherwood Village. Soldiers marched from house to house, pounding on doors. "Time to pay your taxes!"

Confused villagers stumbled from their homes. Each month they paid taxes to the Sheriff of Nottingham, who owned the land they lived on.

"But we just paid last week," one of them protested.

A sour-faced soldier trotted closer on his horse. It was Guy of Gisborne, the Sheriff's nephew and Chief Guard. "From now on," he sneered, "you pay *every* week."

An hour later, the soldiers rode away. Guy's bag bulged with wedding rings, necklaces and brooches. He smirked. "The Sheriff *will* be pleased with me."

Just then, an arrow whizzed past his face and hit a tree. A shadowy figure appeared in the branches.

"An outlaw!" Guy shuddered.

"Not just any outlaw," one of the soldiers yelled. "It's Robin Hood!"

The famous outlaw swung to the leafy ground. "At your service," he said, with a bow.

"Arrest him!" Guy cried.

But the soldiers were too scared. Robin Hood was the most wanted outlaw in England, but also the most dangerous.

"You've been stealing from the villagers," Robin said, spotting Guy's heavy bag of loot.

"We can take what we want," Guy snapped. "The Sheriff owns this land."

"No," Robin replied, "the *King* owns this land."

"Ha!" Guy scoffed. "The King is fighting overseas. He will probably never return. Soon the Sheriff of Nottingham will be king. And you, Robin Hood, will be dead!"

Guy swung his sword. The blade sliced Robin's hand.

Fast as a flash, Robin fired an arrow. It caught Guy's tunic, pinning him against a tree.

The soldiers drew their swords. But now Robin's gang burst from the bushes and bashed them all on the head.

Robin Hood stepped closer to Guy. "Tell the Sheriff," he said, "that as long as he steals from the villagers, I will steal from him."

Guy closed his eyes in fear. When he looked again, Robin Hood was gone. And so was Guy's bag.

Chapter 2

The Sheriff's plan

"Imbecile!"

The Sheriff of Nottingham hurled a cup of wine across the hall of Nottingham Castle. The drink splashed all over Guy of Gisborne's terrified face.

"Once again Robin Hood has made a fool of you," the Sheriff said, pouring himself more wine.

"He made a fool of your soldiers too, uncle," Guy spluttered.

"Be quiet!"

The Sheriff sighed, stroking his pointy beard. "Follow me," he said.

The Sheriff led Guy down a gloomy corridor and unlocked a rusty iron door.

Inside, the room was full of coins. There were bags of gold coins, boxes of silver coins and piles of pennies on the floor.

"This is enough money to make me king," the Sheriff said, sipping his wine. "I fear Robin Hood will steal it. Clearly you can't stop him, Guy."

"I did cut his hand, uncle..."

"I said be quiet! No – I will hold a tournament to find the finest fighter in the land. The winner will become my Chief Guard."

"But uncle," Guy muttered, "*I* am your Chief Guard."

The Sheriff took another sip of wine. Then he hurled the cup again at Guy.

The following day, Robin Hood and his gang held a feast for the villagers at their hideout in Sherwood Forest.

Little John cooked rabbit stew, Will Scarlet baked blackberry pies, and Friar Tuck poured all of the villagers a drink.

As the villagers gathered around the crackling fire, Robin gave them back the loot stolen by the Sheriff's men.

But Robin was worried. Guy of Gisborne had said the Sheriff wanted to become king. It was possible too, if the Sheriff had enough money.

Robin was desperate to stop him, but how? The Sheriff kept all of his treasure safely guarded in Nottingham Castle.

"God bless Robin Hood!" said a villager. "He's the best fighter in all of England."

"He should enter the Sheriff's tournament," another joked.

Robin looked up. "What tournament?" he asked.

A villager handed him a poster.

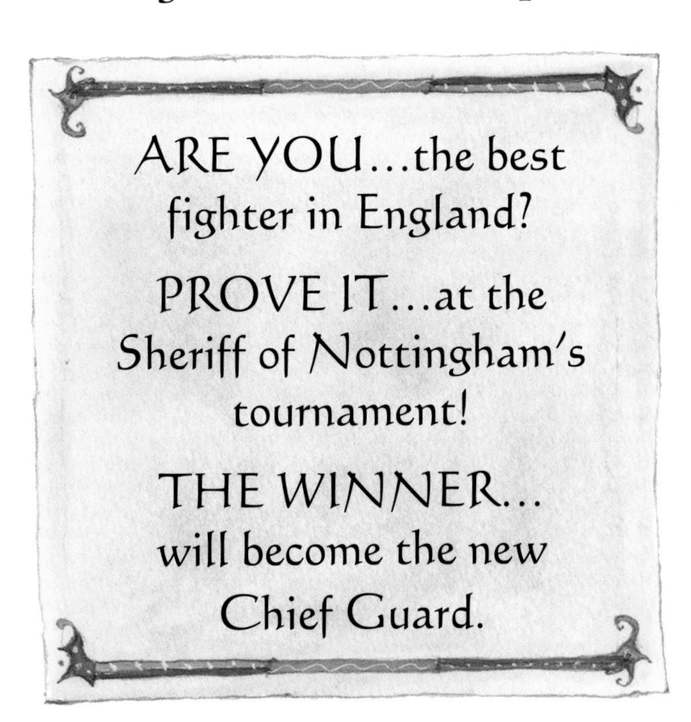

Robin smiled. If he won the Sheriff's tournament, maybe he'd get a chance to swipe his treasure.

Little John guessed what he was thinking. "You can't enter, Robin," he said. "You'll be recognized!"

Robin's grin grew wider. "Not necessarily..."

Chapter 3

Tournament day

Word spread fast about the Sheriff's tournament. Knights rode from all over England, eager to show off their fighting skills. Even the famous Black Knight turned up. Everyone expected him to win.

The first round was sword fighting. Steel blades clashed and clanged – but no one could beat the Black Knight.

"Who's next?" he asked.

"I'll try," a voice called.

A farmer stepped from the crowd. He had a muddy face and a bushy black beard. No one knew it was Robin Hood in disguise.

The duel began, and the crowd fell silent.

Robin twisted and turned. He ducked and dived. He swept away his opponent's legs, and the Black Knight clattered to the ground.

The second round was fighting with sticks. Robin and the Black Knight balanced on a log over the castle moat.

Clash! Bash! Smack! Their sticks crashed together.

As Robin ducked a swipe, his fake beard slipped on his face. Just for a second, he lowered his stick to straighten it...

The Black Knight seized his chance. He whacked Robin off the log and into the moat.

It was all down to the archery contest. They each had two shots at the target.

The Black Knight fired first. *Thwack!*

"Bullseye!" he said.

Robin fired next. *Thwack!*

Robin hit the bullseye too, only his arrow was closer to the middle.

The Black Knight laughed. "Watch this," he said. *Thwack!*

His arrow hit the target dead in the middle. Surely there was no way Robin could win now?

Robin breathed in deeply, and fired. His arrow hit the Black Knight's – and split it straight down the middle!

The crowd went crazy. They had never seen such skill. Even the Black Knight was impressed.

Only the Sheriff of Nottingham wasn't smiling. "Enough of this," he said, dragging Robin away. "Now that you are my Chief Guard, there is work to do."

Beneath his fake beard, Robin grinned. Finally he could get his hands on the Sheriff's treasure.

Chapter 4

The treasure room

The door to the treasure room swung open with a rusty creak. Robin stared in amazement. He had never seen so much money. There was definitely enough here for the Sheriff to become king.

“Your job is simple,” the Sheriff said. “I am convinced Robin Hood will try to steal this treasure. So, as my Chief Guard, you must never leave this room.”

The Sheriff was right – Robin *was* going to try to steal the treasure. But how? Soldiers guarded the corridor, and the only window was barely wide enough to fire an arrow through.

To carry the treasure off, Robin needed an excuse to leave the room.

"What if I'm hungry?" he asked.

"Guy will bring you a pie."

"What if I need the toilet?"

The Sheriff pointed to a hole in the wall. "Over there. Now be quiet and do your job!"

With that, the Sheriff swept off down the corridor.

As Robin gazed around the room, he suddenly realized how he could steal the treasure. He wrapped a message around an arrow and fired it through the narrow window. He hoped his gang would see the shot.

"Why did you fire that arrow?" a voice said.

Guy of Gisborne stood in the door, holding a steaming pie.

"Just being prepared," Robin replied, casually. "Robin Hood could strike at any moment."

Guy was about to boast that he had cut Robin Hood on the hand.

But, as he handed over the pie, he saw the very same cut on the farmer's hand.

With a shudder, he realized that this man *was* Robin Hood. Guy decided to stay quiet. He would wait until the time was right – and then he would strike.

Chapter 5

Thieves in the night

It was the middle of the night. An owl hooted. Moonlight rippled on the castle moat.

Little John, Will Scarlet and Friar Tuck crept up to the water's edge. They had seen Robin's message. It told them to come at midnight and to bring fishing rods.

Quietly, Friar Tuck cast the line into the moat. He wiggled the rod until... "Got one!" he whispered.

He tugged the line, and a bag of coins rose from the water. It was the Sheriff's treasure.

Little John caught another bag. Then Will Scarlet caught one too. But where had it all come from?

Up in the castle, Robin Hood couldn't help laughing. Stealing the Sheriff's treasure had been easy. He simply dropped the bags down the toilet. They fell down a shaft and splashed into the moat.

Outside, Will Scarlet plucked the last bag from the water. "Let's get out of here," he whispered.

Guy of Gisborne burst from behind a bush. "You're not going anywhere," he growled.

Soldiers surrounded Robin's gang. They were caught.

At the same time, more soldiers stormed to the castle's treasure room. But Robin Hood was gone.

The Sheriff was furious when he found out that Robin had escaped. "Where is he?" he demanded from the prisoners. But the three outlaws wouldn't say.

"At least you still have your money uncle," said Guy. "And all thanks to me."

"Yes, yes," the Sheriff said, "but what about Robin Hood?"

"Surely he will try to rescue his gang, uncle. And when he does, we'll catch him."

A cruel smile spread across the Sheriff's face. "You may not be such an imbecile after all Guy," he said. "Hang his gang tomorrow!"

Chapter 6

Hanging day

All night, the sounds of hammering and sawing echoed around the castle courtyard. The Sheriff's soldiers built a wooden scaffold with ropes tied around the top.

This was where Robin's gang would be hanged.

By morning, dark clouds swirled over Nottingham Castle. Villagers gathered in the courtyard, glancing anxiously around the high walls. They prayed that Robin Hood would save his friends.

A drum roll rumbled around the castle walls. Soldiers marched the prisoners from the dungeon.

Friar Tuck stumbled over, but Little John and Will Scarlet helped him stand. They refused to show the Sheriff that they were scared.

"Long live the King!" Little John cried out.

"Down with the Sheriff!" yelled Will Scarlet.

"God bless Robin Hood!" Friar Tuck bellowed.

The crowd cheered. But where *was* Robin Hood? He was running out of time to save his friends...

The soldiers dragged the prisoners onto the scaffold. A hangman looped ropes around their necks.

Beneath the prisoners, the scaffold floor swung away. The three men dangled in the air, struggling desperately for breath.

The crowd could barely watch. Robin's gang only had seconds left to live...

Thunder roared. Lightning streaked across the sky. An outlaw appeared on the castle wall.

"Robin Hood!" someone cried.

But the famous outlaw was too far away. How could he save his gang from there?

Robin raised his bow and fired a single arrow. It shot over the crowd's heads – and sliced through all three of the hangman's ropes.

Robin's gang tumbled to the ground. Soldiers rushed to grab them, but the villagers blocked their path.

"Forget the prisoners!" screamed the Sheriff.

Guy of Gisborne led the soldiers up onto the castle wall. They surrounded Robin from both sides. Swords trembled in their hands.

Robin fought bravely, but even he couldn't beat so many soldiers. A blade cut his arm. Another struck his side. With a desperate cry, he fell from the wall...

...and into the castle moat. The water turned red with blood.

The soldiers waited to see if the outlaw rose to the surface. A minute passed. And then another. But Robin didn't rise.

"Robin Hood is dead!" Guy declared triumphantly.

"You imbecile," the Sheriff cried. "Look!"

High at the top of the castle stood Robin Hood! And he had the Sheriff's treasure.

Guy stared at the outlaw, then at the moat. He didn't understand. "How did he do it?" he said.

Chapter 7

How Robin did it

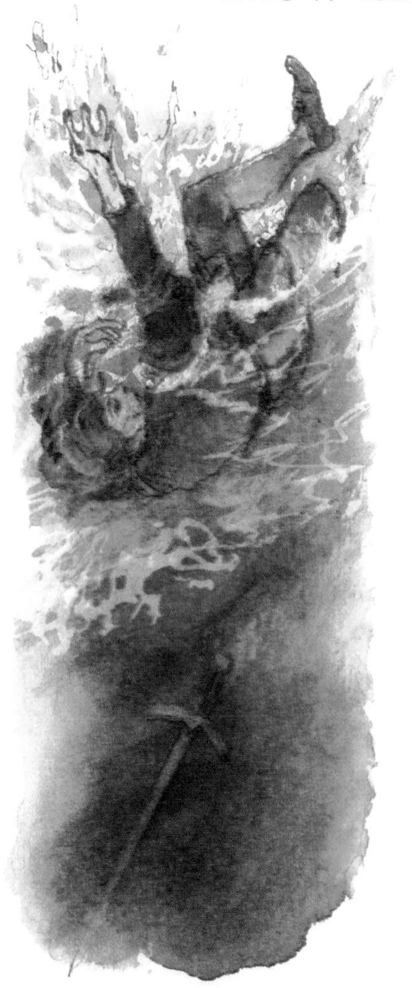

How did Robin escape the moat? And how did he get the Sheriff's treasure? This is how...

Robin plunged into the castle moat. Blood gushed from his wounded arm. He sank deeper in the murky water.

High above, he saw the blurry shapes of soldiers on the castle wall. If he swam up to the surface the soldiers would catch him – or kill him.

How could he escape? Then Robin remembered – the toilet!

Frantically, he swam underwater, feeling for the hole to the toilet shaft. His lungs burned. He was running out of breath...

There it was!

Robin burst through the gap and rose, gasping, into the vile shaft.

Moving fast, he wedged himself into the narrow space. He pressed his feet against one wall and his back against the other. Then he began to climb, higher and higher up into the castle.

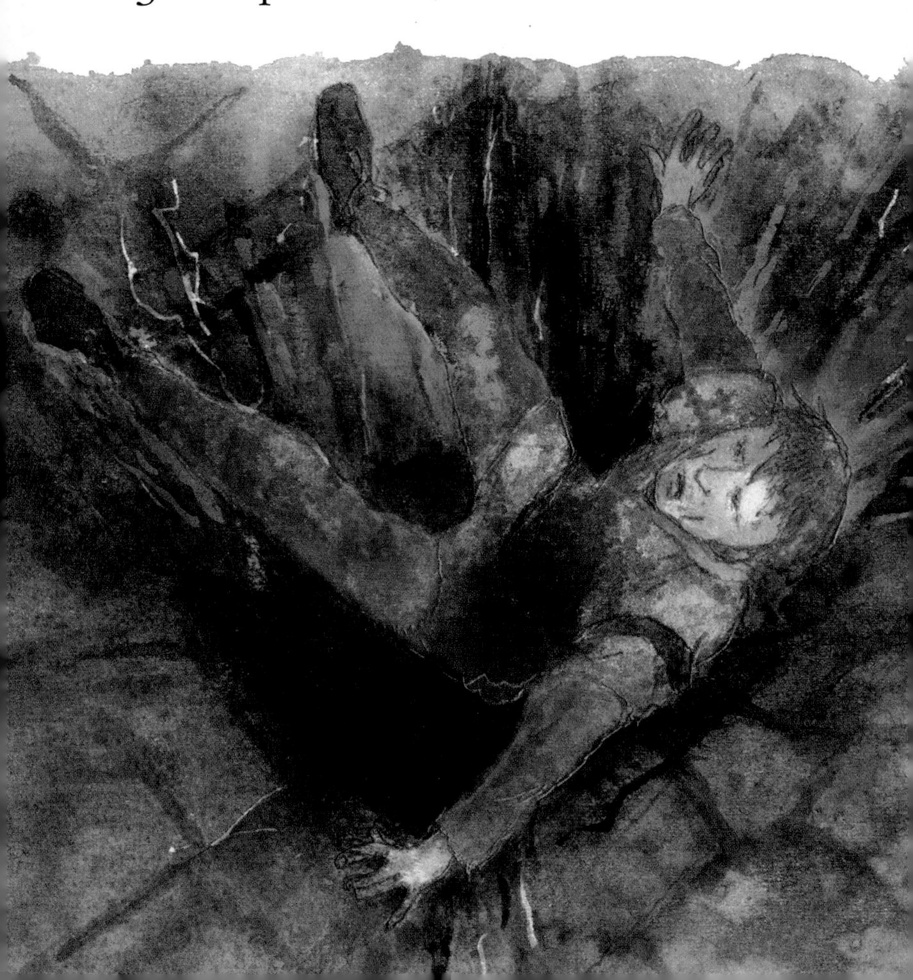

Groaning with effort, Robin clambered into the Sheriff's treasure room. A guard attacked, but Robin whacked him on the head.

He stole the Sheriff's treasure...

...and dragged it outside.

Now, raising the heavy sack, Robin tipped all of the treasure down into the castle courtyard.

Gold and silver coins showered below. Delighted villagers snatched them up, filling their pockets.

"Stop them!" the Sheriff cried. "Save my treasure!"

But Robin's gang blocked their way, and the soldiers didn't fight back. They were fed up with working for the greedy Sheriff.

"Imbeciles!" the Sheriff roared. "I'll stop them myself."

But before the Sheriff could draw his sword, Robin shot an arrow from his bow. It caught the Sheriff's cloak and pinned him to the wall.

Robin fired again. His next arrow struck the wall inches above the Sheriff's head. A message unrolled from the shaft, and hung right in front of the Sheriff's face...

The Sheriff of Nottingham trembled with rage. "Stop Robin Hood!" he screamed. "Save my treasure!"

But his treasure was gone.

And so was Robin Hood.

About the story

No one really knows if Robin Hood ever existed, although there was a Sheriff of Nottingham during the Middle Ages, and a huge forest in Sherwood. Outlaws lived there in secret hideouts. Some became popular heroes, because they fought back against corrupt officials. Villagers told stories about an outlaw they called Robin Hood. These stories became legend.

Designed by Michelle Lawrence
Digital design: Nick Wakeford
Series editor: Lesley Sims
Series designer: Russell Punter

First published in 2011 by Usborne Publishing Ltd.,
83-85 Saffron Hill, London EC1N 8RT, England.
www.usborne.com

UE. First published in America in 2011.